D0786344

Remember
the Butterflies

by Anna Grossnickle Hines

DUTTON CHILDREN'S BOOKS

NEW YORK

Published in the United States by
Dutton Children's Books,
a division of Penguin Books USA Inc.

Designer: Susan Phillips

Printed in Hong Kong by South China Printing Co.
First Edition   10 9 8 7 6 5 4 3 2 1

Library of Congress Cataloging-in-Publication Data
Hines, Anna Grossnickle.
   Remember the butterflies/by Anna Grossnickle
Hines.—1st ed.
      p.   cm.
   Summary: When Grandpa dies, Holly and Glen
remember the special times they had together—
gardening, reading, and learning about butterflies.
   ISBN 0-525-44679-6
   [1. Death—Fiction.   2. Butterflies—Fiction.
3. Grandfathers—Fiction.]   I. Title.
PZ7.H572Re   1991
[E]—dc20   90-3536   CIP   AC

In loving memory of four very special grandfathers—
Paul Grossnickle, Joe Putman, Howard Finn, and
Earl Grossnickle, whose grandchildren will know him
only through the memories of others.

Holly found a butterfly by the forget-me-nots in her grandfather's garden. It lay still in her hand.

Glen tried to help it fly, but it wouldn't. "Let's take it to Grandpa," he said. "He knows all about butterflies."

Holly carried the butterfly very carefully.

"It won't fly, Grandpa. Can you fix it?"

Grandpa took the butterfly in his big hand. "Ah, a spring azure." He nudged it with the tip of his finger, but the butterfly didn't move.

"You always fix things," said Holly.

Grandpa shook his head. "This butterfly was a living thing. I can't fix living things that die."

"It's still so pretty," said Glen. "I wish it wasn't dead."

"You know," said Grandpa, "I'm sure it laid some eggs before it died. The eggs will hatch into little caterpillars, and the caterpillars will change into more butterflies, and those butterflies will lay more eggs."

"I want to see the eggs," said Holly.

"So do I," said Glen. "Where are they? Can we see them?"

"Butterfly eggs are very, very tiny," Grandpa said. "And my old eyes don't spot things as well as they used to. But your eyes are young and sharp. We can certainly look."

Holly and Glen followed their grandfather into the garden. Holly brought the butterfly.

"Spring azure eggs are green, if I remember correctly," Grandpa said. "Tiny, tiny green bumps. The butterflies like to lay them on the dogwood buds or wild lilac blossoms, so the little caterpillars will have plenty to eat when they hatch."

They looked on the buds of the dogwood tree and on the wild lilac bush, but they couldn't find any eggs. Not even one.

"Maybe there aren't any," Glen said.

"Oh, yes, there are," said Grandpa. "We might not be looking at the right buds, or the eggs might be so well hidden that we just can't see them. But before you know it, lots of little caterpillars will be crawling around, eating the blossoms and getting fat."

"Too bad we can't find your babies, butterfly," Holly said.

Glen looked at Holly's hand. "Maybe we should leave the butterfly in the garden with Grandpa's flowers. Right here. See? It's just the same color as the baby blue-eyes."

Holly lay the butterfly very gently on the flowers. She softly touched one of its wings to say good-bye. Then she looked at the blue dust on the tip of her finger.

"Let's celebrate the butterfly's life," Grandpa suggested. "We'll remember how beautiful it was, and we'll be glad that its life will go on and on because of the eggs it left behind."

"Just imagine what it would be like," Grandpa said, "if all the flowers turned into butterflies, flying all around us."

Glen squinted so he could see the colors dancing through his eyelashes. "I can see them, Grandpa. I can see all the butterflies."

"See, Holly? Watch me. I'm dancing with the butterflies."

Holly danced, too. And they pretended they were butterflies. Their grandfather helped them fly.

During the summer, they saw lots of butterflies in Grandpa's garden. Orange and yellow sulphurs, cabbage whites, silvery blues, and some with lots of colors like painted ladies and tiger swallowtails. Grandpa showed them the different caterpillars and the holes they ate in the leaves and blossoms of his plants.

In the fall, they found a golden brown chrysalis hanging from a branch of the dogwood tree. Grandpa said there was a caterpillar inside that would change into a butterfly over the winter. When spring came, there would be a new blue azure in the garden.

In the winter, when the snow fell, Holly and Glen
built a snowman by the wild lilac bush. Grandpa
watched from the window. He said the cold was
too hard on his old bones.

But afterward he made hot cocoa for them and read stories aloud from a big green book. Lots of times that winter, Grandpa fell asleep in his chair.

Then, one cold day, Grandpa died. Friends and neighbors came to the house dressed in dark, sad colors. Some people cried. They all remembered things they loved about Grandpa.

Glen and Holly remembered too, and they missed him.

In the spring, the crocus and the grape hyacinths came up in Grandpa's garden. So did the weeds. "I think Grandpa's garden misses him," Mother said.

Holly and Glen helped her pull the weeds, just as they'd helped Grandpa. Together they planted forget-me-nots, pansies, bachelor's buttons, and snapdragons. "Grandpa's favorites," Mother said.

Soon the first blossoms appeared on the dogwood tree. The chrysalis was still there, but now it was open. "The butterfly came out," said Glen. "Just like Grandpa said. Let's try to find it."

Holly and Glen looked carefully all over. "Look!" Holly said suddenly. "There it is! There's a spring azure! Maybe it's the one."

"I bet it is," said Glen. "Grandpa said its life would go on and on because of the eggs. He was right."

"I wish Grandpa could see it," said Holly.

"You know, Grandpa's life will go on and on, too," said Mother.

"How?" Holly asked. "He didn't leave any eggs behind."

"He left his garden," Mother said. "And he left us. I'm his child, and you're my children, and someday you may have children, and that will go on and on."

Then Holly and Glen remembered all the special things about Grandpa: working with him in the garden; sitting on his lap and feeling his scratchy whiskers; listening to him read stories from the big green book; and watching him wink at them over his coffee cup.

"And Grandpa taught us about butterflies," said Holly. "We danced with the butterflies and the flowers, and he helped us fly. We had a celebration."

"Let's do it again," said Glen.

And they did. They danced, and they helped each other fly. And they sang, "We love you, Grandpa. We love you and the butterflies, and we'll always remember."